DUDLEY PUBLIC LIBRARIES

The loan of this book may be renewed if not required by other readers, by contacting the library from which it was borrowed.

D0716066

To Lucy,
who was the first
to go to Pluto

Letter to Pluto
An original concept by author Lou Treleaven
© Lou Treleaven

Illustrations by Lou Treleaven
Cover illustrations by Katie Abey

Published by MAVERICK ARTS PUBLISHING LTD
Studio 3a, City Business Centre, 6 Brighton Road,
Horsham, West Sussex, RH13 5BB
+44 (0) 1403 256941
© Maverick Arts Publishing Limited October 2016

A CIP catalogue record for this book is available
at the British Library.

ISBN: 978-1-84886-231-9

Printed and bound in Great Britain by
Marston Book Services Ltd, Oxfordshire

Letter to Pluto

By Lou Treleaven

URANUS

It's brrrilliant!

The coldest planet in the Solar System, Uranus is perfect for your next skiing holiday.

Wrap up warm and give it a try!

Can you escape the deadly Blarg-ringed flapper?

Find out on Neptune!

Come to Neptune's water parks and try some fun sports while weird creatures lurk beneath the waves!

Pluto

Small, smelly and far away.
DON'T BOTHER.

Class 5H

Northcroft School

England

Earth

Tuesday 10th January 2317

Dear Straxi

Our teacher Mrs Hall wants us to write a letter to someone on another planet. I've got you. I didn't know anyone even lived on Pluto.

"What's a letter?" I asked Mrs Hall. "You need a pen, paper, and an envelope," Mrs Hall said. She is !

writing to a head teacher on Mars
about ~~nit~~ knitting patterns. I've got
nothing to say about knitting. So Mrs
Hall said to tell you about my family.
"Who'd want to know about them," I
said, but Mrs Hall said I had to get on
with it or stay in at break, so here
goes.

MY FAMILY

My big brother. He looks
like this when he's chasing
me. Scary.

Little sis. Always happy.
About everything. No one knows why.

 Dad. He mends computers.
He likes taking things apart
for fun.

Mum. Her name is
Dawn. She has a
gardening ~~busn~~ business
called Dawn's Lawns. I asked her
yesterday what she would have done
for a job if she hadn't been called
Dawn. She gave me a funny look.

I'm stopping now as my hand is
aching. Mrs Hall says we have to
keep writing, it is a dying art. !

"Good, let it die," I said, and then she said, "You are staying in at break Jon Fisher."

Jon

Class 5U

Flumpenslurp Blurble School

Dome 1

Pluto

Fiveday 13th Gagarin 2317

Dear Jon

Thank you for your letter. It was funny. I've never had a letter and didn't know what to expect. It wasn't that! You told me all about your family, so here is mine.

STRAXI'S FAMILY

My gran. She is the head teacher at my school.

Imagine living with your head teacher.
Imagine walking to school with your
head teacher.

Mum and Dad. They run a
café called Doolyboppers and we
live above it. My dad is well
known as he has a weird
hairstyle that has never caught
on (yet)! Mum's grandparents were the
first people to move to Pluto from Earth.
Their names are carved on to a stone
spaceship in the town square. Fame!

My twin, Bryd. She's always
around. She's even leaning over me as I

write this letter. GO AWAY BRYD!

These are my pets. I have two pimpams
and a striped zork. Actually I don't as
we can't have pets living above the cafe.
So I have imaginary pets instead. They
are very well trained, apart
from the zork which
keeps sitting on my head.

You forgot to draw a picture of yourself.
If you want to know what I'm like, look
at the drawing of Bryd. She's just like
me.

Straxi

13

Class 5H

Northcroft School

England

Earth

Tuesday 17th January 2317

Dear Straxi

Mrs Hall marked our letters out of
ten for neatness. She gave mine a
four. I thought she'd be pleased to
read all that stuff about herself but
no. She gave yours a nine.

My gran would make a very bad head
teacher. She went planet-hopping
when Grandad died and enjoys it so

much she hasn't come home yet.

Gran likes writing by hand just as much as Mrs Hall and is always sending us postcards that take weeks to get here. The last one was a postcard of a giant snail on Jupiter. By the time we got it, she'd left and gone to Neptune. Dad said the snail could have got to us faster than that postcard.

← slime

I don't know how people ever wrote letters like these all the time. My hand is going to fall off and then Mrs Hall will be sorry.

Mrs Hall said in the old days they
used to write with quills dipped in ink.
The quills were made out of feathers
sharpened at the end. "Why weren't
the birds all bald then?" I asked, and
Mrs Hall told me to stop being so silly
and did I want to miss break again.

Jon

PS Why did you say you looked just
like your twin — she is a girl!

Class 5U

Flumpenslurp Blurble School

Dome 1

Pluto

Fiveday 20th Gagarin 2317

Dear Jon

Of course I am a girl! What did you think I was, a blue-headed skwitch? Do you have them on Earth? We have loads on Pluto. They are giant birds, with six foot long feathers - that's one whole dad. I asked my dad to build a bird table in the garden for

One dad

one feather

them but they squashed
it flat. And him, because
he was underneath it
putting the last nail in.
But he is okay now.

Your gran sounds great. I'd love to
planet hop. I've never even left Pluto.

I like the idea of writing with a feather.
Did people really do that? And did the
birds go bald in the end? I would have
knitted them jumpers in return. It's
only **fair**.

Straxi

Class 5H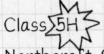

Northcroft School

England

Earth

Tuesday 24th January 2317

Dear Straxi

I asked Mrs Hall if I could swap
penpals but she said there weren't
any more boys to go round. I said I
didn't want to write to a girl on Pluto
which it turns out isn't even a proper
planet. But she said, "Straxi sounds
like a very interesting person to me."

Rex Smith's penpal collects old toothbrushes, so perhaps she's right.

Then Mrs Hall said, "Why don't you find out a bit more about quills?" so I did. Then she said, "How interesting Jon, why don't you write a report about it?" and I cursed deep inside my head where she couldn't hear and said, "Yes okay why not."

So here is a copy of it in the envelope and you can read it and make it into a paper aeroplane if you like.

And then Mrs Hall did a surprising thing as she came up to me with a present. It is a pen which looks like a quill but it's really a biro and I'm writing with it now!

I'm keeping the quill at school in my drawer. If my big brother knew I was writing to a girl on Pluto with a quill he'd die laughing.

Jon

A HISTORY OF QUILLS by Jon Fisher

A quill is a pen made out of a feather, which seems a bit random. I mean, why a feather, why not a stick? ✔

Interesting start Jon

Anyway, turns out there is a reason which is not just the nice fluffy bits at the end which flap about making you look like Shakespeare, but also the inside is hollow and filled with ink. ✔ Not while it's on the bird though or it wouldn't be able to take off. Also it could write its name in the sky if it did manage to take off.

What's the difference between a quill and my brother? One is full of ink, and the other (guess which) is full of stink.

Not appropriate Jon.

Quills were really popular in the Middle Ages ✔ and loads of people had them, especially monks who liked to draw in the margins of their books which isn't allowed today, worst luck.

Then metal pens were invented and everyone decided they would pay for them and not pick them up for free off the ground which is weird. Oh, except for some artists who still like writing in old styles for fun.

Remember to keep on the subject!

Quills have a rank like football teams where swan is the top followed by goose, and right down the list is turkey. ✓ I would like to try writing with a peacock feather — it would be huge and good for big things like motorway signs. *Better...*

If you are right-handed you should use a feather from a bird's left wing and if you are left-handed you should use one from their right wing. ✓ A good way to remember this is to imagine you are shaking hands with a bird.

Lovely picture.

An interesting if rather short history of quills.

Try to report the facts rather than your own train of thought. Mrs Hall.

Class 5U

Flumpenslurp Blurble School

Dome 1

Pluto

Fiveday 27th Gagarin 2317

Dear Jon

I don't know about Earth, but here on
Pluto you can be friends with anyone.
One of mine and Bryd's best friends is a
boy and he's bright blue. But I guess it's
different on Earth.

I asked Miss Urdlepun - that's my
teacher - if I could swap penpals too, but
she said there must be something we

have in common even if we are from different planets.

So I thought hard and here's a list of things we have in common.

1. We both have penpals! Okay, that's a bit silly.

2. We both have mad grans. Not everyone does, believe it or not.

3. We both hate vomblefruit. (That's just a guess. But everyone hates vomblefruit, right?) Phewee!

4. We both like quills. Yours sounds cool.
I wish I had one.

Straxi

P.S. I also have an imaginary zork on
my head but Bryd says that's not
normal.

Class 5H

Northcroft School

England

Earth

Tuesday 31th January 2317

Dear Straxi

Mrs Hall liked your list. She said, "Why don't you write back about that, Jon, instead of staring into space?" so here goes.

1. We both have penpals! So does everyone in my class. Well, nearly everyone. Rex Smith got banned. I don't know what he wrote but Mrs Hall tore up

his letter and put in the bin.

2. We both have mad grans. Gran has sent me a photo of her surfing on Neptune, wearing a hello earth t-shirt.

3. We both hate vomblefruit. What is vomblefruit? If everyone hates them then they sound a bit like brussel sprouts which are the colour of sick and evil.

evil
sprout

4. We both like quills. If you like quills you will like this because guess what? I am sending you the quill in case my brother finds out about it. Actually you've probably already seen it in the

envelope. So this is the last
sentence I will ever write
with a quill.

Apart from this one,
goodbye.

Jon

(And that one.)

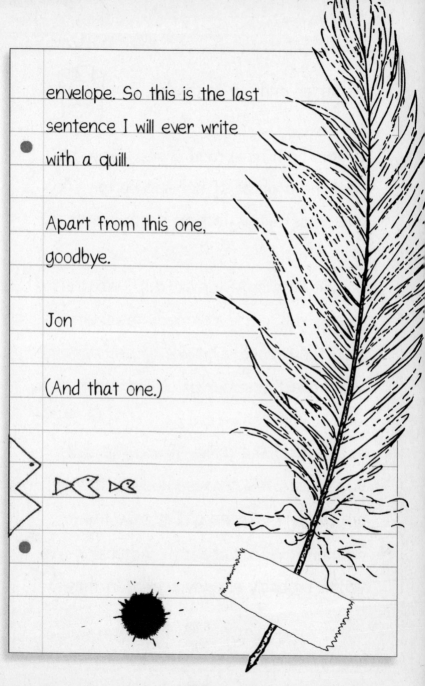

Class 5U

Flumpenslurp Blurble School

Dome 1

Pluto

Fiveday 3rd Fiennes 2317

Dear Jon

Thank you for the quill which I am writing with right now.

It makes me think I'm in the olden days on Earth when people lived in castles and shot arrows at each other (twang!) and didn't even know Pluto was here. I would send you a blue-headed skwitch feather but they are six feet long (or

about one dad) and hard to fit in an
envelope.

So instead I am sending you a
vomblefruit so you can see for yourself
how horrible they are.

Make sure you peel it outside so you
don't stink everybody out. Then take a
bite. A big one!

Straxi

THE VOMBLEFRUIT COOKBOOK

By Ursula Copperbottom

Take the 'vom' out of vomblefruit with these mouth-watering recipes!

Includes:

Vomblefruit pie
Vomblefruit smoothie
Vomblefruit tart with vomblefruit whip
Roast vomblefruit on a bed of vomblefruit
with vomblefruit sauce

You won't believe it's got vomblefruit in it!
(unless you taste it)

The Vomblefruit Cookbook © Ursula Copperbottom
Published by PLUTO PRESS LTD
52, Main Street, Dome 1, Pluto, Outer Solar System
© Pluto Press Ltd. 28th Grylls 2305
ISBN: 189-2-95997-298-1

Class 5H

Northcroft School

England

Earth

Tuesday 7th February 2317

Dear Straxi

YEEEUUUCHHH! You're right. I hate
vomblefruit. I tricked big bruv into trying
some, to get him back for all the times
he chases me around the house
pretending to be a monster (he doesn't
have to pretend much). He grabbed it
right out of my hand and took a huge
bite. He now looks like this:

My little sis didn't try the vomblefruit.
She still looks like this:

Dad said to bury it, but
Mum was worried it would grow into a
vomblefruit tree and all our neighbours
would collapse from the smell.

So she has put it in her greenhouse
instead and now she goes and admires it
every day. I suppose it's not bad to look
at now it's too far away to make me
barf.

ewl

Jon

35

Class 5U

Flumpenslurp Blurble School

Dome 1

Pluto

Happyday 11th Fiennes 2317

Dear Jon

I'm glad your Mum kept the vomblefruit.
Tell her to hold it up in the sunlight to
see the colours at their best. Shame it
tastes like a snargler's toothbrush.

A snargler is a blind double-ended slug
thing that lives in swamps. In case you
don't have them on Earth.

I asked Dad why vomblefruit trees don't grow all over Earth too, and he said Earth is four and a half light hours away and has a completely different eco-system, which means plants and stuff.

But guess what? The President of Pluto is trying to get rid of all the smelly vomblefruit trees so more tourists will come. Then maybe you could visit one day and see blue-headed skwitches and snarglers for yourself?

Here's a leaflet about snarglers for you to read. It was put through the door of

the café   by someone in an anorak.

It's the weekend so I'm helping out at Doolyboppers today. Got to go!

Straxi

President of Pluto

Nature walk
and Snargler Count

The society's nature walk will take place next Funday in the Pulsating Swamp. Members will be asked to count how many snarglers they see and record them in their snargler spotters' notebooks. Please bring an anorak and a flask of plubberslurp as we will be pausing mid-swamp for a break.

Know your snarglers!

✔ Tick off the ones you've seen!

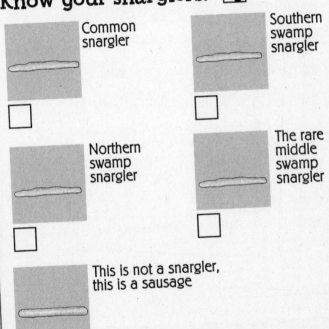

Common snargler ☐

Southern swamp snargler ☐

Northern swamp snargler ☐

The rare middle swamp snargler ☐

This is not a snargler, this is a sausage

Class 5H

Northcroft School

England

Earth

Tuesday 21st February 2317

Dear Straxi

Everyone has gone handwriting mad
because — guess what? WiseUp TV are
coming to school to make a programme
about us! They heard about Mrs Hall
and her mission and they want to film us
all writing to our penpals on other
planets.

Mrs Hall went into a right panic,

panic!

especially when she thought I'd lost the quill which she hoped would look good on the telly. When I told her I'd sent it to you she changed her tune and said, "Jon you are a surprising boy sometimes," to which I had no answer for a change.

It's a good thing I did send you that quill. Otherwise I would have been filmed using it.

Evil Big bruv seeing my quill...

I liked the Snargler Spotters leaflet. They sound like the train spotters we have on Earth.

What work do you do at the café? I asked my mum if I could help her with Dawn's Lawns in the holidays for extra pocket money and she gave me her look.

Then she said she would pay me to stay away. So much for being ~~enter entrep~~ entrepreneurial. (Why can't letters have spellcheck? Mrs Hall you are crazy!!!)

Jon

Class 5U

Flumpenslurp Blurble School

Dome 1

Pluto

Fiveday 24th Fiennes 2317

Dear Jon

Wow, you will be on TV! A famous letter
writer! Make sure you write Straxi
really big when they film you, like this:

STRAXI

And then write about how brilliant I
am! Only joking. Just be normal. Be

yourself. Your letters are funny.

You ask what I do at Doolyboppers. I help Dad serve the food Mum makes. It's mostly Whirlywangs, which are the best desserts ever.

This one is for you. It's got extra yuffs!

Straxi

Class 5H

Northcroft School

England

Earth

Tuesday 28th February 2317

Dear Straxi

They are filming right now! As I write!
Mrs Hall said we can have two merit
marks each if we sit still and write a
good letter. My mind is blank.

Now they will be filming me staring into
space like an idiot and my
brother's face will look like
this:

Great. Now I've drawn my brother's face on telly. I'll cover it with my arm if the cameras get nearer. I'm not having HIM getting famous thanks to me.

Oh yes, STRAXI is a great penpal. She sent me a Whirlywang with extra yuffs. There you go. Your name is on telly.

And now the big news. Gran may get to taste a real Whirlywang because she is going to Pluto! She told me about it on a postcard, so she is probably already there. I told her to go to Doolyboppers and said if she sees a pair of twins in there, you'll be the one holding a quill.

Jon

PS We have just been told to keep writing because Mrs Hall is being interviewed and they want us all working away in the background. So I will just tell you that when she saw I'd written <u>MRS HALL YOU ARE CRAZY</u> at the bottom of my last letter, she TOOK AWAY two merits! And I've just realised I've written it again so that'll be two more.

Mrs Hall you are CRAZY!!!
Jon

Flumpenslurp Blurble School

Dome 1

Pluto

Fiveday 24th Fiennes 2317

Dear Jon

Guess what?

Your gran is sitting right in front of
me in the cafe! I showed
her the quill and she
wants to see me use it, so
I'm writing my next letter
to you.

I hope I can still write to you now you

are a famous person off the telly. I wish I could watch it, but we only get boring old Channel Pluto which is mostly documentaries about gardening in low gravity.

Your gran is great. I can write that now as she's turned away to talk to yes, you guessed it, MY gran! They have got on like a burning yum-yum tree ever since your gran came into the cafe for a Whirlywang three days ago. She seems to know all about me as well!

Your gran says to send you her love, and stop fighting with your brother please, and also she's had a Whirlywang and they are as good as they look, apart from the extra yuffs which are not to everyone's taste.

I DISAGREE!

She is going to do a talk at my school about how she got chased by a blarg-ringed flapper surfing on Neptune.

Your gran was surfing, not the flapper. They just lurk under the surfers getting ready to attack.

Your gran said she only saw one tentacle and a fang and that was enough.

Straxi

The deadly
Blarg-ringed flapper

Class 5H

Northcroft School

England

Earth

Tuesday 7th March 2317

Dear Straxi

Sorry that Gran is going to your school.
I am only related to her a little bit, and
that is just to the non-mad part.
Was the talk good? Did Gran show
everyone her bite marks?

The WiseUp TV programme went out
and I looked like a right snargler in it.

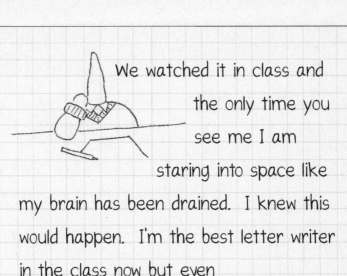

We watched it in class and the only time you see me I am staring into space like my brain has been drained. I knew this would happen. I'm the best letter writer in the class now but even Rex Smith looks like he's got the hang of it more than me.

(He is allowed to write again as long as he sticks to a list of subjects from Mrs Hall.)

Mrs Hall said "The cameras

have put ten years and six pounds on me." I said, "You looked like you always do Mrs Hall," and I could see her itching to take another two merits off me. Then the programme showed her collecting up the letters to post and you could clearly see the bottom of mine where I wrote MRS HALL YOU ARE CRAZY for the second time.

So then she really did take two merits off me. Twice.

Jon

Class 5U

Flumpenslurp Blurble School

Dome 1

Pluto

Fiveday 3rd Mallory 2317

Dear Jon

You are a quarter 'Mad Gran' – that is more than a little bit related!

Your gran's talk was great. She is now a celebrity here. I told you we don't get many tourists. Everyone blames it on the vomblefruit, but I think we are just too far away. The only visitors we get

are scientists and explorers. And mad grans!

Anyway, your gran really is a celebrity and not just because she's the only person wearing gravity boots. (We're used to low gravity and wear slightly heavier clothes.)

Yesterday the President of Pluto took her on a bird-watching trip. They went to see the blue-headed skwitches doing their courtship dance in the Blue Prairies. When they came back to Doolyboppers for a furgel juice afterwards, we heard him say, "You are

quite a lady, Doris," even though she'd brought binoculars with her to watch ten feet high birds which is a bit 'Mad Gran'. Then Bryd said to me, "I bet they get married, dont you?" And it would all be because of us and the letter writing and Mrs Hall's mission.

Straxi

THE BLUE-HEADED SKWITCH COURTSHIP DANCE

Right leg up

Left leg up

Right leg up

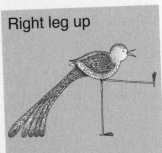

Squawk!

PLUTO NATURE NOTES

One of Pluto's Seven Natural Wonders!

Class 5H

Northcroft School

England

Earth

Tuesday 14th March 2317

Dear Straxi

Mrs Hall said the Pluto government are
spraying the whole of Pluto with
vomblefruit killer. They are going to get
rid of vomblefruit once and for all —
hurray I can hear you shout all the way
from Pluto seven point five billion
kilometres away (look Mrs Hall, I've
learnt something).

Hurray!

Mrs Hall says she won't be able to post my letters because no space shuttles will be going in or out of Pluto until the spraying has finished. "Does that mean I can stop writing?" I asked, but Mrs Hall said, "Absolutely not," and she will save up my letters and post them all at once later on. So I groaned loudly but secretly I was pleased because I like hearing about Doolyboppers and Mad Grans and blue-headed skwitches and even snarglers because they are weird but people like them (like my brother).

So I don't know when you will read this. I don't even know how they can spray a whole planet.

How big is the can?

Do you have to stay inside or do you get
sprayed too?

How long does it take?

Jon

Class 5H

Northcroft School

England

Earth

Tuesday 21ˢᵗ March 2317

Dear Straxi

I haven't heard from you, and you
haven't heard from me as I'm not allowed
to send my letter yet. But it's Literacy,
so here goes.

I watched the news with Dad last night to
see if they said anything about Pluto
being sprayed but they didn't. When he

got over the shock of me
watching the news, Dad
explained that the Pluto
people left Earth because
there were too many

wars and they wanted to start again and
be peaceful. And they were right
because I have never heard of a war on
Pluto. So Earth is ignoring them on
purpose, like little sis does when big bruv
won't play My Ickle Pickle Dress-Up
Princess Pony with her.

Jon

Class 5H
Northcroft School
England
Earth

                              Tuesday 28th March 2317

Dear Straxi

I wonder what's happening? How is Gran
(mine)? The message on the Visit Pluto
website (visitor count 00005) says you've
all got to stay inside for another two
weeks. Two weeks!

Are you bored? Have
all the vomblefruit

trees gone yet? We still have the
vomblefruit you sent. At first the
greenhouse smelt rank, but Mum has
filled it with all the nicest smelling plants
she's got. Also I

WEIRD!!

caught her giving
it a little polish
with a cloth.

Mum claims she
has masked the smell but
every so often I catch a
whiff on her clothes. Eau de
Vomblefruit. That's a fancy
name for a perfume, if
anyone was mad enough to

Eau de
Vomblefruit

make one out of vomblefruit. It would

have to come with a free sick bucket.

I hope you get this letter soon.
I don't draw sick buckets just
for fun, you know.

SICK
BUCKET

Jon

Class 5H

Northcroft School

England

Earth

Tuesday 4th April 2317

Dear Straxi

What is going on!?

I am writing this imagining you sitting at home waiting until it's safe to go outside.

I wonder what your home looks like?
Somewhere that sells Whirlywangs with extra yuffs must be pretty crazy looking.

Talking of crazy looking (and acting),
little sis asked big bruv to cut her hair.
On one side. Mum said her new hairstyle
was punishment enough. Sis said she
was trying to look like My Ickle Pickle
Dress Up Princess Pony with a lovely
mane. And she sort
of does.

Before

Then Mum said, "That
reminds me, Jon, you
need a haircut as you
are beginning to look
like a yeti." (That's a big hairy
monster that lives up
mountains in case you

After

don't have them on Pluto. Actually we
don't have them on Earth either. I think
they are a myth. Or extinct.) I said,
"Why have I got to be punished too?" and
she said, "A haircut isn't a punishment,
Jon, it's a treat, and I wish I could spend
three hours sitting in the hairdressers
instead of pulling up people's weeds and
running around after you children all day."

THREE HOURS?! What do they do, cut
one hair at a time?

I hope you get this letter one day and it
doesn't just live in Mrs Hall's desk forever
like Rex Smith's project on belly button

P.T.O

fluff. I am sending you a yeti.

Jon

A yeti

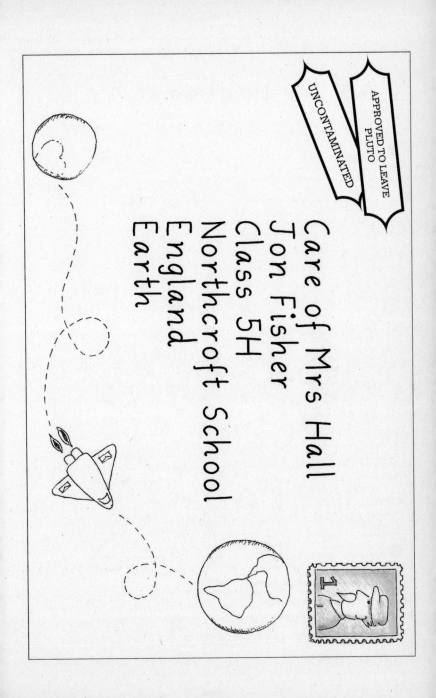

Class 5U

Flumpenslurp Blurble School

Dome 1

Pluto

Fiveday 21st Aldrin 2317

Dear Jon

It's me! At last! Thank you for the yeti
and the perfume and the sick bucket.
They arrived all at once! Sorry I
couldn't tell you what was happening.
They made us stay inside because the
spray wouldn't go away. Bryd said it
was like a big old sneeze hanging in the
air.

We had to do lessons at home with an
e-teacher. That means YAWWN!
the teacher is at her
home and you are at
yours. You can see her
drinking her cup of
buggle-tea and
yawning.

For meals we had to eat packets of dried
space travel food - yuck! Bryd and I
sneaked downstairs to Doolyboppers to
make ourselves Whirlywangs, but Dad
caught us. He said to save the
Whirlywangs for the customers as
everyone will be dying for a treat when

they come out. So we had to resist. We deserve a medal.

Our house is pretty crazy. It has a flashing sign and huge models of food on it. My bedroom has a great view of a giant glowing plastic yuff!

Mum and Dad have a bed on stilts – not fair!

Toilet lift you have to be quick

Me!

Building a wall to keep Bryd away from my stuff

Gran's room

Mum and Dad's room

Bryd watching the Pogs on TV – again!

Dizzy Street

Doolyboppers

MENU

Mum cooks

Dad serves customers

Table and glow lights ready for customers

Chum burgers nearly done!

All the vomblefruit trees are dead, every single one. I feel so sad. Everyone is celebrating saying tourists will come and bring money to Pluto, and then we can build more domes and farms.

But I miss the vomblefruit trees. They were so beautiful, even though the fruit smelt worse than a yeti's underarm.

Straxi

PS Thank you for still writing to me, even though I wasn't writing back.

PPS I drew you a meal from

Doolyboppers and a picture of my house.

PPPS And I wondered if you knew what was happening and if you were thinking about me.

PPPPS You were! You drew me a yeti and some perfume and a sick bucket!

Chum Burger

JON'S SPECIAL MEAL AT DOOLYBOPPERS

Dizzy St, Pluto

Served by the best waitress in the Solar
System, Straxi Dooly!

STARTER
Bugglecrumpet with Melto-Lac cheese and
smippo dip

MAIN
Plip legs and ri tentacles on a bed of wriggle-
shrimps (Only joking, chum burger of course!

DESSERT
Whirlywang surprise
(The surprise is it's double size!)
Best shared with a twin. Or penpal.

Class 5H

Northcroft School

England

Earth

Tuesday 25th April 2317

Dear Straxi

Thanks for the meal. And thanks for
not making me eat ri tentacles. Chum
burger sounds much nicer (I think).

I've been showing everyone the picture of
your house. Gran (mine) is lucky being
on Pluto. I wish I had a toilet lift and
dinner on the ceiling.

We got a postcard from Gran (mine)
today too. I'm writing back to both of
you at the same time - well,
one after the other, not one
with each hand at once.
No, I'm writing TWO
letters today. And I'm
not even at school. Mrs Hall would
probably die of happiness if she saw me.

I looked up Pluto online. Bit bare, isn't it?

Jon

PS   Now I have   I'm sooooooo happy!!
to write to Gran.

PPS She'll want to hear I've been doing something exciting and risk-taking, like her.

PPPS I had to look through the lost property bin for my PE shorts on Thursday.

PPPPS   I'll tell her about that.

LOST PROPERTY

Class 5U

Flumpenslurp Blurble School

Dome 1

Pluto

Fiveday 28th Aldrin 2317

Dear Jon

We don't eat dinner on the ceiling! It's a pull-down table and chairs, to save space. Don't you have furniture on the ceiling?

It does look bare here. And it's so quiet. It's not just the squelch of falling fruit that's missing or the sound of people going, "Yuck!"

The birds are quieter too. I walked right past a blue-headed skwitch yesterday and he just looked at me as if to say, "Oh humans, what have you done?" But Mum said it was probably just looking down at my shoes, which are fluorescent yellow and tasty-looking to birds.

Sad skwitch

So I went upstairs to do my homework, but I kept looking out of the window and

there were no blue-headed skwitches
nesting in the yum-yum tree anymore
and I couldn't even make an imaginary
one in my head.

Straxi

My yellow shoes

Class 5H

Northcroft School

England

Earth

Tuesday 2nd May 2317

Dear Straxi

You have fluorescent yellow shoes?

Maybe they are normal on Pluto. Tip:

they are not normal here.

Don't worry about the birds. They

probably just didn't like the spray. If it

really was like a big sneeze hanging in

the air, I don't blame them.

We have no furniture on the ceiling.

There is some tomato sauce there where little sis shook the bottle without putting the lid back on first. I wonder how long it will stay there or if one day it will drip down on big bruv's head?

Got another postcard from Gran (mine). She said she might be coming home soon. Can you ask her to bring a menu from Doolyboppers? And a feather. I know you can't post one, as they are six

I hope it lands on big bruv

feet long, but surely one would fit on a spaceship?

Mrs Hall has just peered over my shoulder. Now she's asking me to finish my letter and go and help Rex Smith. I don't know if that's a reward or a punishment.

You carrying a feather

Jon

A feather carrying you

Class 5U

Flumpenslurp Blurble School

Dome 1

Pluto

Fiveday 5th McArthur 2317

Dear Jon

The birds have stopped singing. There
is no green anywhere, it's all brown and
dying. I was right to feel sad. The blue-
headed skwitch liked vomblefruit and it
doesn't want to eat anything else.

They said on Pluto News that its
trailing feathers spread pollen around.
Now none of the other plants are

growing either. Even our yum-yum tree
has gone all droopy.

Lots of people are leaving. Your gran's
decided to stay and help. She has a
meeting with the President. I don't
think they are going on dates anymore,
everything is too serious for that.

My quill has run out. It doesn't feel the
same.

Straxi

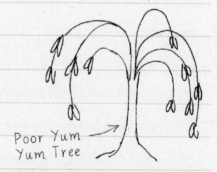

Poor Yum →
Yum Tree

Class 5H

Northcroft School

England

Earth

Tuesday 9th May 2317

Dear Straxi

I've just seen Pluto on the news!
I asked Dad why they were finally
showing stuff about Pluto and he said it
was a disaster now so more interesting
and also people are saying I told you so
because the Pluto Project is a failure. I
asked him what the Pluto Project was
and he said it was about freedom and
also the challenge of survival in a harsh

environment. I think he means like the mouldy shower at school. No one wants to go in there because it smells but Rex Smith stayed in there for ten minutes and got respect.

I asked Mrs Hall where she got the quill from and she said she would get me another one. But now people are leaving Pluto maybe you'll come to Earth soon?

I bet you'll like it. We don't have weird buildings like you do, or giant birds, and you might not want to wear fluorescent yellow shoes. And the gravity will be different. And my brother lives here.

Hang on, that's just going to put you off.

We do have some cool animals here.

Sharks are great. And crocodiles. I like

anything that chases people and bites

them. Apart from my brother, of

course.

Pluto can't really be dying. Can it?

Jon

This is
a shark

This is a
crocodile

(Just in case you didn't know)

Class 5U

Flumpenslurp Blurble School

Dome 1

Pluto

Fiveday 12th McArthur 2317

Dear Jon

Mum and Dad have had to close
Doolyboppers. Everyone is leaving and
too busy packing and booking their
flights to come in and eat Whirlywangs.

Dad doesn't want to go straight to
Earth, he says we'll go to Neptune first
and see the blarg-ringed flapper, and
then we'll visit Uranus and do a tour of

the moons. They made it sound so
exciting, and I've always wanted to leave
Pluto and travel, but now I don't want
to go.

Pimpam

I was going to be the first zoologist on
Pluto and have real pimpams and a fully
trained zork. And Bryd was going to
make Wangywhirls which are like upside-
down Whirlywangs but they won't work
in heavier gravity. Nothing on Pluto will
work anywhere else. It's our home.
Everyone hated the vomblefruit trees
when they were here. We didn't know
they were keeping everything else alive.

The President says the spray was too good, there isn't one single vomblefruit left. They can't even plant any seeds to grow them again.

He has told your gran to go home. Bryd says they can't get married now and they are star-crossed lovers. That means fate is keeping them apart, though I know it's really vomblefruit.

We have invited your gran to come to Neptune with us. I think she wants to get revenge on the blarg-ringed flapper.

Straxi

Like moons? You'll love URANUS

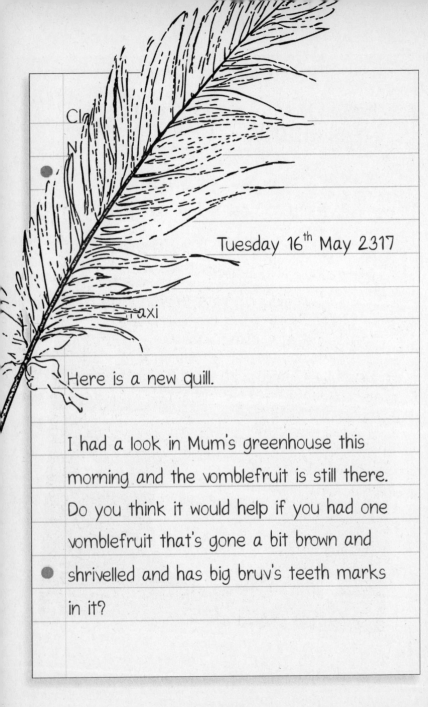

Cl...

N...

Tuesday 16th May 2317

...axi

Here is a new quill.

I had a look in Mum's greenhouse this
morning and the vomblefruit is still there.
Do you think it would help if you had one
vomblefruit that's gone a bit brown and
shrivelled and has big bruv's teeth marks
in it?

I asked Mrs Hall to post this urgently
when I've finished. She gave me a sickly
smile and said, "The way you have taken
this project to heart, Jon, makes all the
years I have put into my teaching career
worthwhile."

"Surely that's worth a few merits," I said.
"We'll see," she said, in a cunning tone
that is meant to bribe me into being
good.

Jon

FBS

Dome 1

Pluto

19 McArthur

Dear Jon

Yes! Yes! Yes!

Get the seed out of the middle of the vomblefruit (hold your nose)! Send it to me! Hurry!

Straxi

98

Same old school

Same old planet

Tuesday

Dear Straxi

The seed is in with this letter. I don't

know how to wrap it so I've just sticky-

taped it to the paper. It's glowing. Hope

that's normal. Also it doesn't really smell

much any more – guess Mum's pongy

plants have helped.

I'm posting this myself as I didn't want to

wait for school. Some things are more

important than Literacy.

SHOCK HORROR!

Mrs Hall must never read that last
sentence.

Jon

FBS

Dome 1

Pluto

26 McArthur

Dear Jon

The seed's arrived! With a police escort!
Flashing lights, sirens and everything! I
can't believe you did all that! The
President hasn't planted it yet. They
are trying to decide the best site and
they are going to fence it off and have a
guard around it day and night. Pluto
News are filming everything! Got to go!

Straxi

Still here

Earth

Tuesday 30th May 2317

Dear Straxi

I didn't arrange anything! I posted the
letter to you with the seed, and when I
got back Mum was weeding the front
garden and said, "Isn't it sad about Pluto?"
I said I'd sent you the seed and she said,
"Eek! That might just work!" but when I
said I'd just sent it in an envelope she
said, "Eek!" again and called our local MP
and he called the Prime Minister. Yes
really!

Then the Prime Minister sent police

around to escort the seed to Pluto, which

sounds important and exciting but trouble

was it was still in the postbox so the

police just had to stand around the

postbox until the postman could come

and unlock it and get the envelope out.

Then a police helicopter came down and

took up the envelope with the seed in it,

and the police went too, and the postman

got accidentally

taken up in the

helicopter as

well, I could see

him waving and
shouting although
I expect he
enjoyed it really.

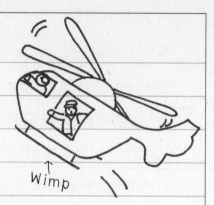

↑
Wimp

Next day I woke up and WiseUp TV
were waiting outside the house to
interview me! I showed them the plan of
Doolyboppers and told them all about you
and the blue-headed skwitches and
Whirlywangs, and the reporter said, "I
didn't know Pluto was so interesting

sonny, I would like to go there some day."
And I said I would too. Then he turned to
the camera and said in a dramatic voice,
"Can one boy save life on Pluto?" Which
I thought was a bit over the top, even
more so when we watched it
later and you could
see Mum putting
her arm round me
and sad music
playing in the
background while they zoomed in on my
gormless face.

I know everyone's supposed to want to be

WHY?!

famous, but now I am I can tell you that fame is just one big embarrassing moment. With witnesses.

Jon

FBS

Dome 1

Pluto

Fiveday 3rd Johnson 2317

Dear Jon

Every day I walk to the planting site. It is surrounded by police from Earth and Guardians, which is the name for our police on Pluto.

There is a special dome over the seed to protect it and a giant video screen showing a close up view. I don't think so many people have ever spent so long

looking at nothing.

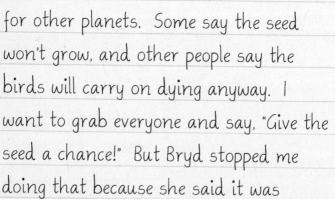

A lot of
people are
still leaving
for other planets. Some say the seed
won't grow, and other people say the
birds will carry on dying anyway. I
want to grab everyone and say, "Give the
seed a chance!" But Bryd stopped me
doing that because she said it was
embarrassing.

Think I'll go and look at the seed again.
I'll stand with the skwitches. They have
the best view.

The reporter was right - if it works we will have SAVED PLUTO!

Straxi

Where?

Over here!

Earth

6 June 2317

Dear Straxi

Reporters are camped outside the house filming my every move. Mum has got loads of new clothes and had a five hour haircut.

5 HOURS?!

Dad took a camera apart for fun and now the reporters don't like him very much. Little sis is putting on a show with her toy ponies and big bruv has stopped chasing me because he doesn't want to look bad on TV in front of his new girlfriend. So things are good. Weird, but good.

Except for one thing. Mrs Hall is trying to get loads more schools to write to penpals on other planets and wants me to be an Ambassador of Handwriting.

"What's that?" I said.

"It means you would be the face of my campaign."

"No thanks," I said, "I would rather eat vomblefruit for breakfast, lunch and tea." Turns out I have no choice and, "It will mean extra merits, Jon, and you know how you like those."

Teacher's pet at last, how I have changed. I will go and tie my brother's shoelaces to the chair leg to make up for it.

And then I'll go and watch the seed on the news.

You can stop now filming now, I've finished. That bit was for the reporters, not you.

I SAID I'VE FINISHED!

Nope, they're going to come with me to the postbox. The burden of being a celebrity.

Jon.

PS Come on seed, you can do it!

FBS

Dome 1

Pluto

Dear Jon

Lots of people have left Pluto now. Only
the people who weren't sure like Mum
and Dad are holding on just in case.

Everyone who's still here is visiting the
seed but it's me, Bryd and the Mad
Grans who are there the most.

More and more skwitches are standing
around near the planting site. I think

they are waiting and hoping, just like us.
If we can stay on Pluto I would like to
study them. I might even go and live in
a flock for a while. Bryd says I'm weird
but that's what I would like to do. And I
already have the shoes.

Yes, I did say Mad Grans with an s.

Your gran refused to leave. She says she can help and besides, she likes the vibe here. "What's that?" I asked. "Is it a nickname for the President?" as she sometimes calls him funny names like poppet. She blushed and said, "No, it's something everyone has on Pluto and it makes me want to stay."
I wonder if all grans are mad or if it's just ours?

I've got the seed a present. It's a little pebble from the Glowing Canyon. I'm going to put it just outside the dome so

it has to stretch
out of its little
hole to see it.

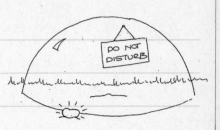

Off to the planting site now. Wish you
could come with me.

Straxi

PS   Just got back - it's poking out of
the ground! And it's got two leaves! We
did it! We did it! Running to the post
box right now!!!

Guess...

Yes! Earth!

13 June 2317

Dear Straxi

We did it! We really did it!

So this is the last letter I will write to you. At least for a while. Because...
I'M COMING TO PLUTO!

"How? When? Why?" you are asking. Well, stop asking and I'll tell you.

WiseUp TV came to school yesterday to

interview me about how our letters have saved Pluto (nearly). But your letters were at home and mine were on Pluto so that was going to be a very short programme.

Then Mrs Hall rushed over to her laptop and turns out she scans in everybody's letters before she sends them so she can mark our spelling and punctuation. Nosiness is what I call it.

She won't like reading that. Sorry, Mrs Hall. Anyway, I don't care because

I'M COMING TO PLUTO!

So, after they had filmed bits of the letters and I saw my pictures of perfume bottles and you on a feather, I wished I could disappear. But then the

reporter handed me an envelope, and inside were return tickets to Pluto and there were five. One each for me, Mum, Dad, big bruv and little sis. I tried to drop my brother's ticket on the floor but the reporter thought it had slipped out of my hand in all the excitement and gave it back to me. 😐😲

We are coming out next week! WiseUp TV are coming too and they want to film me and you standing in front of the tiny tree. IT'S A TREE!

Earth news is showing loads of Pluto stuff now. They said they are going to follow the story and Earth is going to do more to support Pluto, even though the Pluto people left Earth to start again on their own. And then they showed the President

of Pluto saying forgive and forget, and I
saw Gran (mine) next to him wearing her
hello earth t-shirt, and I saw two twins
waving like crazy and one was holding a
quill and I knew it was you.

Jon

Max 26C, min 9C   19ᵗʰ Johnson 2317   £1

SEED OF FRIENDSHIP SAVES 'PLANET' PLUTO

Penpals plot a plan to post Pluto seed!

Jon (Earth) and Straxi (Pluto) save the 'planet' of Pluto when they plot a plan to post the last vomblefruit seed in existence from Jon's greenhouse back to Pluto.

Pluto's president had decided to eradicate the smelly vomblefruit trees in hopes that it would increase tourism. "It was a plan that the whole planet supported," the President said, "but we had no idea that it would have such a drastic impact on our ecosystem."

When the 'planet' was on the brink of desertion, young Jon and Straxi came to the rescue. Story continues on page 7.

Blarg-ringed Flapper attacks are on the rise

Neptune coast guard reports an increase in the vicious attacks from the native Blarg-ringed Flapper that lurks near Neptune's popular beaches.

"We've seen a rise in attacks in the last few months and predict more for the summer." says chief watch officer, Robert Urn, "it is tough to put precautions in place due to the creatures' lurking tendancies."

We spoke to a Blarg-ringed Flapper suvivor, Mrs Fisher from Earth, to find out more about these attacks. Here is her story:

"I was surfing at Ariel Beach, which by the way is the best beach for surfing in Neptune, when out of nowhere, I was...

FASHION & BEAUTY

Stylish Anti-Gravity Boots

u de Vomblefruit: The of Perfume?

COMMUNITY

Whirlywangs - to yuff or not to yuff?

Adopt a Skwitch!

The End

Jon's first Whirlywang!

Fisher family selfie!

Mad grans selfie!

Lil sis meets a Skwitch

Photobomb!

Brothers and sisters selfie

Classic!

It's a tree!!

Northcroft School

England

Earth

Tuesday 21 June 2317

Dear Jon,

I have not received your first letter yet, but I am
hoping you enjoyed your flight to Pluto. Why don't
you write and tell me about it using lots of describing
words?

Mrs Hall

Northcroft School

England

Earth

Tuesday 28 June 2317

Dear Jon,

I am disappointed not to have received a letter from
you yet. I know the solar postal system is slow, but
Rex Smith still managed to receive his weekly jigsaw
piece from Uranus. (How he thinks he and his
penpal can do a jigsaw together by post is beyond
me.) I look forward to hearing all about your first
week.

Mrs Hall

Northcroft School

England

Earth

Tuesday 5 July 2317

Dear Jon,

I have just seen you on Solar System News eating a

Whirlywang. Please send me your first letter or I

will take away 2 merits, which will be very difficult

as you don't have any. I am enclosing a homework

timetable. And don't forget to write a holiday diary.

And a thank you letter to the TV people. You are my

Ambassador of Handwriting now, remember? I hope

you are actually reading this, Jon. Jon?

Mrs Hall